I AM READING

The Giant Postman

SALLY GRINDLEY

Illustrated by

WENDY SMITH

KINGFISHER

For Postman Martin – S.G.
To R & P – W.S.

KINGFISHER
An imprint of Kingfisher Publications Plc
New Penderel House, 283-288 High Holborn
London WC1V 7HZ
www.kingfisherpub.com

First published by Kingfisher 2000
This edition published 2007
2 4 6 8 10 9 7 5 3 1

A CIP catalogue record for this book is available from the British Library.

ISBN 978 0 7534 1483 5

Printed in China
1TR/0107/WKT/(CG)/115MA/C

Contents

Chapter One

"He's coming!" screamed a little girl.

"He's coming!" shouted the
ice cream man.

"He's coming!" shouted
the window cleaner.

Children dropped their
school bags and ran.

Shoppers dropped their
shopping and ran.

Joggers stopped their
jogging and RAN.

Soon, the street was empty.

It was so quiet you could hear a pin drop.

Then there was a loud thump.

And another. And another.

THUMP! THUMP! THUMP!

Great big boots cracked the

pavements.

Great big boots shook the houses.

Behind closed curtains, people

shivered with fear.

"Please don't have any post for us,"

they whispered.

THUMP! THUMP! THUMP!

The Giant Postman was coming.

Chapter Two

Billy and his mum lived at Number 24.

"Get under the table!" screamed
Billy's mum.

But Billy stood at the window
and watched the Giant Postman
stomping from door to door.

THUMP! THUMP! THUMP!

The Giant Postman was right outside
Billy's house.

BANG! BANG! BANG!

He bashed on the door.

"I've got a parcel for you,"

he bellowed.

"Just leave it
outside, please,"
called Billy's mum.
"Oh no," replied
the Giant Postman.
"I don't want it
to be stolen."

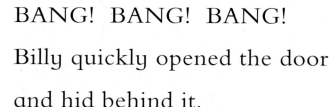

BANG! BANG! BANG!
Billy quickly opened the door
and hid behind it.

"Here you are!"
bellowed the
Giant Postman
and he dropped
the parcel on
to the floor.

Then he stomped off down the street.

THUMP! THUMP! THUMP!

"Has he gone?" whispered Billy's mum.

Billy peeped round the door.

"Yes, he's gone," he said.

Then Billy walked out into the street.

The street was still empty.

Mr White's garden gate was hanging off its hinges.

Mr Homer's cabbages were trampled to the ground.

Mrs Atwell's cat was on the roof of her house, quivering with fright.

One by one the villagers appeared. "Is it safe?" they asked.

"Yes," said Billy, "he's gone.

But it's time we did something.

Getting letters is supposed to be fun."

"We're all too scared to do anything,"

they said.

14

"Well, I'm not," said Billy.

"I'm going to write the postman

a letter and ask him to stop

frightening us."

The crowd gasped.

"And I'm going to deliver it myself!"

Chapter Three

That very day, Billy sat down and wrote his letter.

Dear Mr Postman,
My name is Billy and I live in the village.
I am writing to ask you to stop frightening us, please.

Mr Homer is very upset about his
cabbages and Mrs Atwell's cat
won't come down from the roof.
We would like to be friends
with you.
Best wishes,
Billy

He wrote "Mr Postman"
on an envelope and
put the letter inside.
Then Billy set off
towards the woods where
the Giant Postman lived.
"Don't go, Billy!" cried
his mum.

BY HAND
Mr Postman
The Woods

"Don't go, Billy!" cried the villagers.

But Billy kept on going,

past the baker's . . .

past the shoe shop . . .

past the school . . .

on and on until at last he reached
the woods.

19

The woods were very dark.

Billy heard strange noises.

CRICK! CRACK! RUSTLE!

He began to feel frightened.

CRICK!

He wanted to go back.

CRACK!

But he made himself go on.

RUSTLE!

Faster and faster he went, until . . .

at last he came to a clearing.

There stood the Giant Postman's

great big house.

Billy was surprised to see that

the garden was full of flowers.

He walked up to the door.

Chapter Four

TAP! TAP! TAP!

Billy knocked on the Giant

Postman's door.

Nobody came.

TAP! TAP! TAP!

He knocked a little louder.

At last, he heard footsteps –

SHUFFLE, SHUFFLE, SHUFFLE.

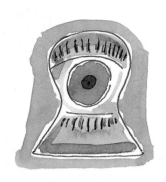

Then Billy saw a giant
eye peeping through
the keyhole.

"What do you want?"
bellowed the Giant Postman.

"I've b–b–brought a letter,"
Billy stammered.

"What do you mean?" said the
Giant Postman.

"I deliver the letters."

"It's a letter for
you," said Billy.

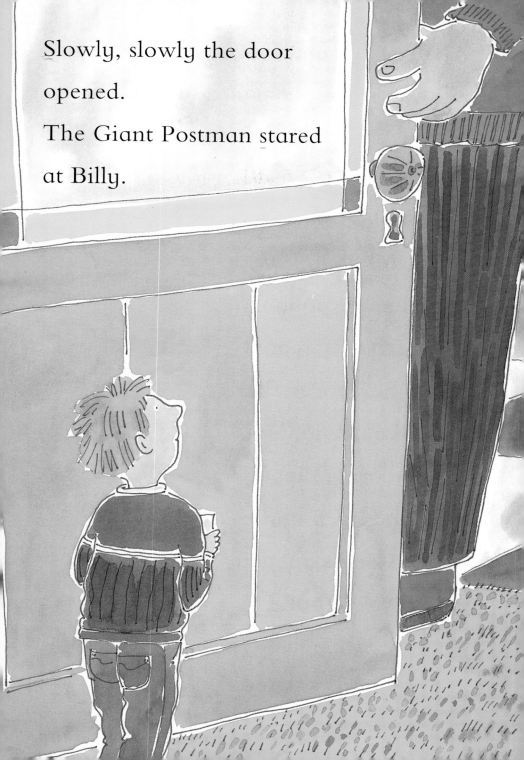

Slowly, slowly the door
opened.
The Giant Postman stared
at Billy.

He took the envelope and peered at it.

Slowly, slowly he pulled out the letter.

He read it, over and over again.

Billy shifted his feet nervously
on the doorstep.

He was all alone with
the Giant Postman.

Billy felt very scared.

Then he noticed that
the Giant Postman
was wearing slippers
and had holes in the
elbows of his jumper.

Billy looked at his
face and thought
he saw him smile.

But the Giant Postman turned away
and closed the door without a word.

Billy ran all the way home,
through the dark woods . . .
on and on until at last he reached
his house.

"Oh Billy!" cried his mum.

"Thank goodness you're safe."

"He read my letter," said Billy,

"but he didn't say a word.

I hope I haven't made him angry."

But that night Billy remembered
the garden full of flowers.
He remembered the slippers,
and the woolly jumper with holes.
The Giant Postman didn't seem
so frightening without his uniform
and his great big boots.

Chapter Five

The next morning, Billy looked
out of his window.

It wasn't long before he saw
people running to hide.

THUMP! THUMP! THUMP!

The Giant Postman was coming.

Great big boots cracked the
pavements.

Great big boots shook the houses.

THUMP! THUMP! THUMP!

The Giant Postman was right outside
Billy's house.

"Get under the table!" screamed
Billy's mum.

But Billy opened the window.

"Good morning, Mr Postman," he said.

From his sack the Giant Postman pulled
an enormous envelope.

"I've got a letter for you," he said.

Then he stomped off down the empty street.

THUMP! THUMP! THUMP!

Billy ran downstairs.

His hands shook as he took the letter out of the envelope.

He read:

Dear Billy,
Thank you for your letter.
I've never had one before.
I don't mean to frighten
people. I'm sorry about
Mr Homer's cabbages.
I'm afraid I'm a bit
clumsy in my boots.
Will you write to me
again tomorrow, please?
It's my birthday.

Your friend,
Mr Postman

Billy smiled and ran out into
the street.

"It's all right," he said, waving
the letter. "You can come out."
He danced up and down
until a crowd had gathered
round him.

Then he showed them the letter.

"Never had a letter!"
said Mr Homer.

"Poor thing,"
said Mrs Atwell.

"He sounds a
bit lonely,"
said Mr White.

"I don't think he's scary
at all," said a little girl.
"I'm going to make him
a birthday card."

"I suppose he can't help being clumsy in his big boots," said Billy.
Just then, he had an idea.

Chapter Six

That night the villagers didn't sleep.
Lights burned in all the houses.
Delicious smells came from the
baker's, and loud noises came
from the shoe shop –
BANG! THUMP! RRRRR!

Up and down the street,
people climbed ladders
and tied knots.

Just as dawn broke, everything was
ready.

The villagers stood by their windows
and waited. And waited.

THUMP! THUMP! THUMP!

The Giant Postman was coming.

THUMP!

THUMP!

The great big boots
stopped in their tracks.

The Giant Postman
stared.

And stared.

Banners and balloons hung from
every house and from every lamppost.
The banners read:

TO OUR POSTMAN, A VERY
HAPPY BIRTHDAY!

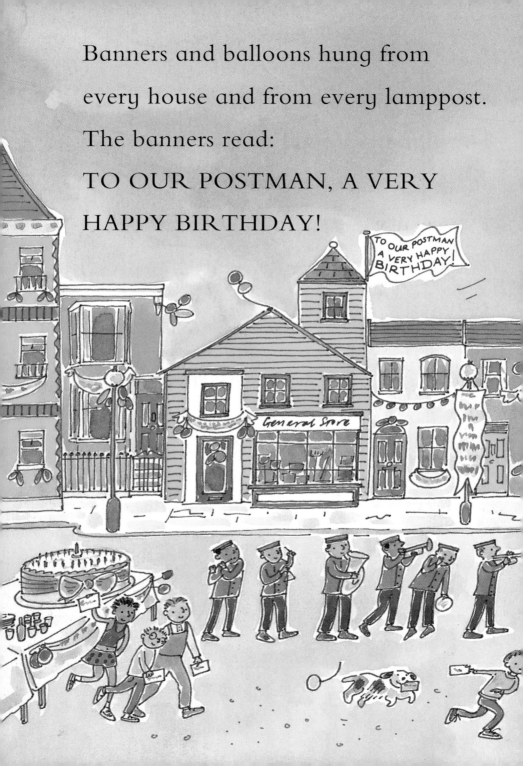

The village band began to play.

DRUM! DRUM! DRUM!

TOOT! TOOT! TOOT-TOOT!

The villagers rushed out into the

street, waving birthday cards.

Billy came out of the shoe shop
pulling a cart. On top of the
cart was the biggest parcel
you have ever seen.

"HAPPY BIRTHDAY,
MR POSTMAN," said Billy.

"This present is from all of us."

Gently, the Giant Postman pulled
off the paper and lifted the lid of
the great big box.

"Just what I've always wanted!"
he gasped.

The Giant Postman held up a

great big pair of new trainers.

"Try them on!" the villagers cried.

So he tried them on.

"They're perfect," he said.

"They're so soft and springy."

He walked up and down

without a single THUMP.

Then the Giant Postman
smiled a great big smile.
The villagers cheered.

"Time for a party," Billy yelled.

"Time for a party," everyone cried.

The Giant Postman danced down

the street.

"Time for a party!" he bellowed

with delight.

"This is the very best birthday ever!"

About the Author and Illustrator

Sally Grindley is an award-winning writer. Her own postman is not at all like the clumsy Giant Postman – he hates having to knock on the door to deliver a parcel. "He always comes early," says Sally, "and he knows I'm embarrassed by my just-got-out-of-bed, crumple-faced, tangle-haired state." Sally Grindley's other books for Kingfisher include *What Are Friends For?* and *What Will I Do Without You?*

Wendy Smith has written and illustrated lots of books for children, and also teaches art and illustration at Brighton University. Wendy says, "I love to hear the letterbox rattle in the morning. I enjoy guessing who the letter is from, and wondering what news I'm going to read!"

Tips for Beginner Readers

1. Think about the cover and the title of the book. What do you think it will be about? While you are reading, think about what might happen next and why.

2. As you read, ask yourself if what you're reading makes sense. If it doesn't, try rereading or look at the pictures for clues.

3. If there is a word that you do not know, look carefully at the letters, sounds and word parts that you do know. Blend the sounds to read the word. Is this a word you know? Does it make sense in the sentence?

4. Think about the characters, where the story takes place, and the problems the characters in the story faced. What are the important ideas in the beginning, middle and end of the story?

5. Ask yourself questions like:
Did you like the story?
Why or why not?
How did the author make it fun to read?
How well did you understand it?

Maybe you can understand the story better if you read it again!